MORE RULES FOR

PERFECTION

(ALMOST)!

Project Best Friend
Private List for Camp Success

PENELOPE PERFECT

LUCKY JARS & BROKEN PROMISES

Chrissie Perry

ALADDIN

NEW YORK LONDON TORONTO SYDNEY NEW DELHI

ALADDIN

An imprint of Simon & Schuster Children's Publishing Division
1230 Avenue of the Americas, New York, New York 10020
This Aladdin paperback edition August 2017
Text copyright © 2015 by Chrissie Perry
Interior illustrations copyright © 2015 by Hardie Grant Egmont
Interior series design copyright © 2015 by Hardie Grant Egmont
Published by arrangement with Hardie Grant Egmont
Originally published in Australia in 2015 by Hardie Grant Egmont
Cover illustration copyright © 2017 by Marta Kissi
Also available in an Aladdin hardcover edition.
All rights reserved, including the right of reproduction in whole or
in part in any form.
ALADDIN and related logo are registered trademarks of Simon & Schuster, Inc.
For information about special discounts for bulk purchases, please
contact Simon & Schuster Special Sales at 1-866-506-1949 or
business@simonandschuster.com.
The Simon & Schuster Speakers Bureau can bring authors to your live
event. For more information or to book an event contact the
Simon & Schuster Speakers Bureau at 1-866-248-3049 or visit our
website at www.simonspeakers.com.
Cover designed by Laura Lyn DiSiena
The text of this book was set in Aldine 401 BT Std.
Manufactured in the United States of America 0717 OFF
10 9 8 7 6 5 4 3 2 1
Library of Congress Control Number 2017942088
ISBN 978-1-4814-9088-7 (hc)
ISBN 978-1-4814-9087-0 (pbk)
ISBN 978-1-4814-9089-4 (eBook)

LUCKY JARS & BROKEN PROMISES

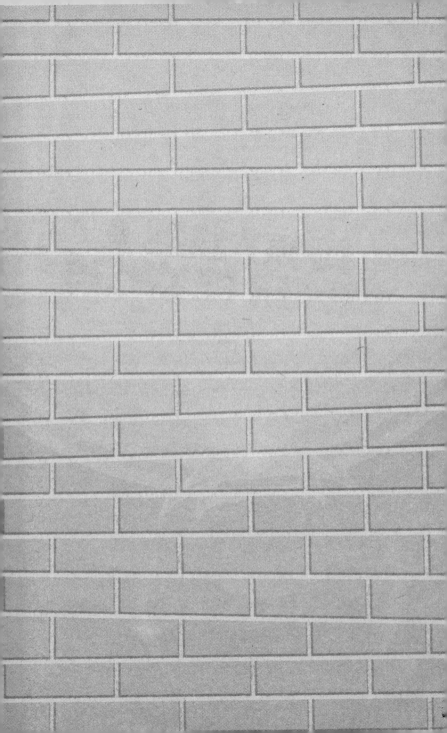

CHAPTER

Family was very important to Penelope Kingston. She often thought about the expression *family ties*, because her family ties had to stretch a rather long distance. You see, Penelope's dad had a new family, and they lived in another state.

Penelope loved her weekly Skype sessions with her dad. He usually called on Thursdays at 5:20 p.m., between work and his regular squash game. The first fifteen minutes were totally for Penelope, and the second fifteen minutes were supposed to be for her brother, Harry. But lately Harry hadn't always shown up for his turn.

This worried Penelope. Didn't Harry realize how important family ties were? Especially really stretchy ones like theirs. But on the *positive* side, Harry skipping his turn meant Penelope got an extra fifteen minutes of her dad—all to herself.

While Harry checked that the sound and picture were working, Penelope prepared for the call. She gathered all of her latest schoolwork and put it in a neat pile on her dressing table. Then she did an extra tidy-up around her bedroom, making sure it would look as organized as the study her dad called from. She brushed her hair, smoothed the creases in her shirt, and double-checked that there was nothing stuck in her teeth. It was *essential* to be absolutely ready and sitting at the dressing table with the laptop in front of her by five fifteen p.m. Six weeks ago, her dad had called four minutes early, while Penelope was in the bathroom. He had left a message on Skype.

Sorry I missed you. I'll try again next week. Dad x

When they finally Skyped a whole week later, Penelope had almost certainly forgotten some of the very important things that had happened the previous week. In fact, she had a hollow, antsy feeling about all her lost news. All the things her dad would never know about her. Since then, she'd kept a list of important events in her iPhone, just in case.

Penelope was absolutely ready and sitting

at her dressing table when the Skype call came through. In one corner of the screen, she could see herself. The biggest area, though, was taken up by her father. He had already changed into his squash gear. Penelope preferred seeing him in a suit and tie, but even in sports gear he looked neat, tidy, and very well-groomed.

Suddenly, she had a flash of him trimming his nose hair in their bathroom.

Penelope's memories of living with her dad were strange that way. Penelope couldn't remember anything about the day he left them for good, but she could remember him trimming his nose hair! (Penelope did not—as far as she could tell—have nose hair, but if she did she would most likely trim it too.)

As Penelope listened to her dad talk, she looked at the books on the shelf behind him.

She wanted to check if they were still arranged in alphabetical order. They were. (Penelope's own books were currently organized by color. She made a mental note to tell him this.)

Really, the two of them were *extremely* similar. Sometimes (and this was an absolute secret), Penelope wondered what it would be like to live with her dad and his new family. Whenever she thought about this, she pictured herself sitting at her dad's desk while he looked through her excellent school reports, nodding his approval.

IT WAS A VERY PLEASANT IMAGE.

Sometimes Penelope's Very Pleasant Images grew into Lovely Daydreams, but this one never did. It was always interrupted by a Very Big Worry about her mum and Harry. How would they get along without her?

She loved her mum and Harry, but they were messy and disorganized. Without Penelope around to look after things, who knew what would become of them?

Her dad took off his glasses, polished them, and put them back on. "My goodness, Penelope Kingston," he said. "Have you grown?"

Penelope shook her head. Because she sat up very straight, people often made the mistake of thinking that she was quite tall. Until she stood up. When she was standing, *NOBODY* made that mistake.

"I have been *trying* to grow, Dad," she explained. "I've been eating growing-type foods and I even did stretching at a Pilates class with Mum the other week. But Ms. Pike has a wall chart in our classroom and she measures us every month. I'm the only one who hasn't grown. For two whole months!"

Penelope paused for a moment before adding the next bit. It felt like a slightly mean thing to say. "I think some people have been cheating, though." Rita Azul had been wearing new shoes on measuring day, and they had seemed Very Chunky.

Plus, Penelope had a strong suspicion that Joanna (the naughtiest girl in the class) had been standing on tiptoe when Ms. Pike measured her.

Just then, Penelope had a thought. It wasn't very nice, but unfortunately Penelope was no more in control of her thoughts than she was of her memories, or her height. The thought was that her very best friend Bob had sticky-up hair that really should have been flattened before Ms. Pike did her measuring. Still, there was no doubt that Bob had grown. They had been almost exactly the same height when Bob first arrived at Chelsea Primary. Now, Bob was a whole head taller than Penelope (not even including her sticky-up hair).

"Well, Penelope, if kids aren't being honest, they're only cheating themselves," her dad said. "Perhaps you should see a doctor. I'll suggest it to your mother."

Penelope had mixed feelings about this idea. On the one hand, it was nice to be taken seriously about not growing. Her mum didn't take it seriously at all. Even Grandpa George (who was excellent to discuss most things with) just told her to let things happen in their own time.

On the other hand, her mum almost certainly wouldn't like her dad's suggestion. Her dad made quite a lot of suggestions that her mum didn't like.

"Sienna is quite tall for her age," Penelope's dad said. Sienna was Penelope's half sister. "She's in the seventieth percentile."

Penelope wasn't sure what a percentile was, but whatever it was, Sienna was obviously doing well on it, and her dad seemed very pleased.

Penelope quickly held her schoolwork up to the screen so he could be happy about that instead. So far this year, except for P.E., she had received nothing but As and A+s. It was very nice to share that with him (even if it was over Skype and not while she was sitting at his actual desk).

"You'll make me broke when you get your report," he said proudly.

Penelope smiled. She knew he was joking.

Still, if things stayed on track, her report would be worth $140 ($20 for each A), which was a Very Good and Welcome thought.

"Also, I have some news!" Penelope said. She waited a moment so her dad could let his excitement build up. "Our school fair is in just two weeks. And I'm on the Lucky Jar committee!"

Penelope and Oscar Finley had been asked to organize the Lucky Jars because of their excellent work on charity days. **Penelope had been honored to be asked.** Lucky Jars were often the biggest seller (after cotton candy, of course). Which wasn't a surprise. A regular, empty glass jar could look Very Enticing once it was decorated and had an assortment of lollies and trinkets inside.

Saying she was on the Lucky Jar commit-tee wasn't completely correct. The words just snuck out of Penelope's mouth. She wasn't entirely sure you could call two people a committee. But she *did* know that her dad (who was a politician and getting quite famous) was on several committees, so she suspected he would approve.

"That's terrific, Penelope!" her dad said, confirming her suspicion. "I wish your brother would take a leaf from your book."

Penelope didn't know exactly what that meant, but she could guess. And just as her dad said it, Harry came into Penelope's bedroom. At the moment, Harry's hair was even longer than Penelope's bob. It was tied in a ponytail. He had mud down one of his legs, most likely from playing soccer.

It was 5:36 p.m., which meant it was Harry's turn to Skype, but Harry whispered that she could stay. **Penelope was pleased.** Even though he had mud on his leg, she moved over so he could share her chair.

"Harry," their dad said, "what's your news?"

"Nothing much," Harry replied.

Penelope bit her lip. Their father waited, but it seemed that Harry was going to stop right there.

Penelope decided to continue for him. "Harry's soccer team is in the grand final!" she said. "Which just happens to be on the same weekend as the Chelsea Primary fair, only on the Sunday."

"Well, well, well. Good on you, Harry," their dad said. "It sounds like an important weekend all around. Can you both wait a moment?" He moved away from the computer and out of sight.

Penelope clicked the stopwatch on her iPhone to measure the time he was off the screen. It was eleven seconds until he returned.

"It looks like I'll be in town for work on the Friday of that weekend," he said. "So how about I get a hotel for the Saturday night? The three of us can go to the fair and the soccer game—and have a mini holiday together!"

"Yes. Yes! YES, PLEASE," Penelope said.

Beside her, Harry shrugged. Penelope wished Harry wouldn't do that. Shrugging was NOT a good thing for stretchy family ties—particularly when there was talk of mini holidays. She didn't want their dad to think that Harry didn't care about spending time with him. Penelope could tell that Harry was actually quite excited by the way he was tapping his foot very quickly on the carpet.

"You might want to get a haircut before then, Harry," their dad said.

Harry stopped his foot-tapping then, and

started to wriggle around as though he was about to stand up. Penelope knew that he hated being told to get his hair cut. But just at that moment Sienna came into their dad's study and climbed up on his lap. Harry stopped wriggling.

Sienna was wearing a hat with bunny ears and eating what looked to be a bubble gum-flavored ice cream (even though it was quite close to dinnertime and Penelope was abso-

lutely sure her dad had been very strict about that sort of thing when he lived with them).

It was also cute when she pushed her face up to the

STILL, THAT HAT WAS EXTREMELY CUTE.

screen and sang "Old MacDonald Had a Farm," with their father suggesting animal after animal to keep her going.

If the rest of the Skype session was about Sienna counting to ten (several times, and always missing the five and eight, even though their dad kept interrupting to remind her) that was also *fine*. And if Penelope didn't get to tell her dad about her books currently being organized by color, that was okay too.

Penelope would have *PLENTY* of time to share everything with her dad when he visited. She was quite sure that Harry's team was going to win the grand final. Plus (and this was the best bit), there was a good chance that she and Oscar Finley would break the school record for the number of Lucky Jars sold at the fair. **When a record was broken at the fair, it was announced over the** loudspeaker. That would certainly impress her dad.

Also, Penelope would finally get to show him the jewelry she'd made for the craft stall. She'd been making some very intricate pieces lately. Her best piece was a bow-tie badge, made with modeling clay. It was amazingly neat around the edges. Her ladybird pendant was a close second.

"I'm going to give this to Dad, absolutely for free, when he visits," Penelope told Harry after the Skype call had finished. She pointed at the bow-tie badge on her jewelry stand. "Don't you think it will look perfect on his business suits?"

Harry stood up but didn't say anything.

"I bet he's going to book a *fancy* hotel too," Penelope continued. "Will it have a pool and a spa, you think?"

Harry wasn't very good at showing his

excitement. Instead of staying to talk to Penelope about hotel spas, he turned and started walking out of her bedroom.

"You'll be able to show him your soccer moves too!" she added.

Harry paused as he got to the doorway, and turned around. He opened his mouth as if he was going to say something, then closed it again. Sometimes Harry was slow at finding words.

"Sure, Penelope," he said eventually. Penelope couldn't understand why he didn't seem excited about the mini holiday they'd just planned.

Penelope wasn't much of a dancer, but when Harry left, she got up and spun around her room.

The three of them were going to have a great time together! Her dad would probably want to start having mini holidays like this all the time.

Maybe it would become a regular thing. It was even possible that he would regret leaving them in the first place.

CHAPTER

2

On Friday, Penelope sat on the bench seats by the basketball court eating lunch with Bob (Penelope's very best friend) and Tilly. Since they'd shared a hut on school camp, Tilly had started to sit with Penelope and Bob quite a bit.

Penelope was chewing on a carrot and conjuring up Pleasant Images. After yesterday's Skype call, she had a new Pleasant Image—her dad lifting her up on his shoulders and walking around the fair. A *lot* of people stared at them because they recognized Penelope's (quite) famous dad from being on TV. Some kids (including the absolutely most popular girl in the entire school, Ellen Semorac) even asked for his autograph. Luckily, Penelope was able to pass her dad a pen she'd been carrying in her pocket.

ELLEN SEMORAC SHOWED HER APPRECIATION WITH A LOVELY SMILE.

Of course, Penelope knew she was too old to be lifted onto her father's shoulders, and it would be embarrassing if it actually happened. But it was a nice image.

Tilly had barely reacted when Penelope told them her dad was coming to town for the weekend, and Bob had just groaned about her own dad volunteering at the cotton candy stand. Neither of them seemed to understand how special it was going to be for Penelope to have her dad for the *whole weekend*. People whose dads lived with them never really got it.

"This is the perfect place for seeing who's crushing on who," Tilly said.

Even though it interrupted her Pleasant Image, Penelope started on her little packet of raisins and concentrated on what Tilly was saying.

The girls in their year had recently started

playing basketball with the boys. Penelope suspected it might be a fad. There had been several fads at her school over the years, like swap cards and Yu-Gi-Oh! and Pokémon and yo-yos. In a way, Penelope hoped that playing basketball with the boys was a fad. She wasn't (not even a tiny bit) interested in playing. For one thing, she wasn't exactly sporty. For another thing, there was something a bit gross about bumping around on a court with boys.

Still, she *was* interested in what Tilly knew about crushes. Penelope was normally very good at deducing things. But, for some reason, she didn't seem to understand much about crushes. Although she would never (at least not until she was practically a grown-up) be silly enough to have a crush herself, Penelope at least wanted to understand what they were.

"Joanna and Alex are sooo crazy in love!" Bob said.

She pointed over to the side of the court, where Alex had Joanna in a headlock. They watched as Alex pulled Joanna around in a circle then released her. If anybody tried to put Penelope in a headlock, she would definitely not be pleased. But Tilly was right about Alex and Joanna. They'd even admitted it.

"What about Sarah, Tilly?" Penelope asked. "Do you think she likes anyone?"

Tilly nodded. "Yep," she said. "She likes Felix Unger. It's obvious."

Penelope FROWNED. She could NOT see anything obvious. "Look at how she's watching him," Tilly continued.

"Well," Penelope said, "he *does* have the ball."

It would be extremely hard *not* to watch

Felix Unger at that moment. Felix was *extremely* good at basketball. As he ran up the court, he bounced the ball under his legs and behind his back in a very tricky way.

"True," Bob joined in. "But wait until he *doesn't* have the ball."

Penelope wasn't quite sure what she was waiting for. But soon, Felix passed the ball to Oscar Finley. Oscar Finley was a *terrible* basketball player. In fact, Oscar's bouncing looked dangerous. One minute, the ball was so low to the ground that Penelope suspected no amount of thumping would lift it up again. The next minute, it was (literally) bouncing off Oscar's own chin. It was a great relief when Oscar managed to roll the ball to Alex.

"See? Sarah is *STILL* staring at Felix, even though the ball is nowhere near him now!" Bob exclaimed.

It was true. Sarah seemed frozen to the spot. It was only when Felix glanced her way that Sarah broke her stare, looking down at the ground instead. But Penelope doubted that was proof of a crush. After all, she had just been staring at Oscar Finley and that *definitely* had nothing to do with a crush.

"Poor Sarah," Tilly said. Now Penelope was extremely confused.

"What do you mean?" she asked.

Bob and Tilly looked at each other in a way that was (Penelope had to admit, even though Bob was her very best friend) quite annoying. As though they both knew something Penelope didn't.

"Felix Unger doesn't like her back, Pen," Bob said.

"How could you POSSIBLY know that?" Penelope demanded (a little snappily).

"He hasn't even noticed that Sarah's been staring at him," Tilly said in the type of explaining voice that Penelope used when she was coaching Joanna in math.

Penelope wished Tilly would say something that made sense.

"And in class," Tilly continued, "he just chats to Sarah, no worries. If he *did* like her, he'd tease her or get her in a headlock or something like that."

Penelope was tempted to put her head in her hands and leave it there forever. What Tilly had just said was not even *logical*. In fact, it was the absolute opposite of logical.

TILLY WAS BEING ANNOYING, AND (UNFORTUNATELY) EVEN BOB WAS MAKING PENELOPE FEEL A BIT ANNOYED. Feeling annoyed was something Penelope tried hard to avoid. Penelope was usually calm and sensible.

But sometimes (really not very often at all), when she got very annoyed, another part of Penelope bubbled to the surface. And when it came to the surface, it could (possibly, sometimes) end up in an outburst. Luckily, even though she hadn't grown physically, Penelope had (almost definitely) grown out of having outbursts.

Even so, Penelope was quite glad she had a proper reason to leave. She stood up.

"I actually have a *Lucky Jar committee meeting* to go to," she explained to Tilly and Bob in a patient and even voice.

Penelope thought it was quite special to sit at the table in the staffroom with actual teachers (even if the only two teachers there were right on the other end, reading newspapers). It was one of the perks of helping with charities and fairs. Another perk was nibbling on the three Scotch Finger biscuits that Ms. Pike had snuck them before she went back to the classroom.

LUCKILY, SCOTCH FINGER BISCUITS BREAK IN HALF VERY EASILY.

"I'd like to make loads of Lucky Jars myself," Penelope told Oscar. "But I'm very busy." Penelope paused and thought about all the things she had to do. There were the Lucky Jars, of course. On top of that, this weekend she had the first-Saturday-of-the-month jewelry stall she always set up in front of her house. If it was a busy day (which happened occasionally) she would have to do loads of work to top up her jewelry collection for the craft stall at the fair.

Truly, if she thought about all the things she had to do, Penelope began to feel QUITE STRESSED.

Oscar Finley must have noticed Penelope's stress. For a boy, he was very good at noticing things.

"Penny, don't worry," he said. "There's no way we could do it all ourselves. We'll get the other kids to make some too. We just have to convince them."

Penelope had a nibble of her biscuit.

"We could put a notice in the school newsletter," she suggested.

"Good idea, Pen," Oscar said. "But only parents read the newsletter. We've got to do something to get the kids hyped."

PENELOPE'S NOSTRILS FLARED A LITTLE. It wasn't *only* parents who read the school newsletter. She was (quite) sure she wasn't the only kid at Chelsea Primary to read it from cover to cover.

Oscar shut his eyes tightly, so he didn't notice any nostril flaring. He sometimes did that when he was thinking hard. When he opened them, Penelope could tell he had an idea. **His eyes looked shiny.**

"How about we do a rap at assembly this afternoon?" he said. "A Lucky Jar rap!"

Penelope shook her head and kept it moving from side to side so Oscar would see he absolutely wasn't going to convince her.

"No way," she said. "That would be Truly Terrible."

"Aw, come on, Pen," Oscar urged. "It would be fun. I can do the rap if you don't want to perform onstage. And you're awesome at making up stories, so I reckon you'd come up with something great. Let's just try it, okay?"

Penelope was still shaking her head, but it was getting slower. Oscar was correct about her being good at making up stories.

Oscar breathed deeply and put his hand on his heart (over his school sweater).

"Think of the school, Pen," he said. "We could break the Lucky Jar record!"

Suddenly Penelope had a Pleasant Image of being at the fair with her dad while the announcement was made over the loud-speaker. He would be SO PROUD. Penelope and Oscar had broken several records on important charity days. They were absolutely well known for it (well, among the organizers, at least). It would be amazing to break this one too.

Perhaps she should go with Oscar's suggestion. Sometimes, sacrifices had to be made.

"All right, Oscar," Penelope said (quite graciously, she thought). "Go and get a pen and paper."

CHAPTER

At school assembly that afternoon, Penelope and Oscar lined up for the microphone. It was quite a long wait. First up was a year-one girl tearfully showing pictures of her lost cat. (Unfortunately, the cat she'd drawn looked more like a skunk, so Penelope wasn't sure the pictures would help.) Then a group of students reported their sporting results for the ENTIRE week.

After that, the award certificates were

given out. This week, only two students in Penelope's year received awards. Unfortunately, Penelope was not one of them. But it was a relief, at least, that Alison Cromwell wasn't either. Though Penelope was still the biggest award winner of her entire year, Alison Cromwell was sneaking up behind her. At the moment, Penelope was (fairly) happy with the gap between them (Penelope: 46 awards, Alison: 32), but she definitely had to stay on her toes.

Penelope was quite sure that she should have more than 46 awards. Just this week, she had picked up papers in the courtyard without even being asked. The yard-duty teacher had seen her doing it, but he obviously hadn't reported it to the principal. Penelope had gone to Ms. Bourke's office to let her know what she'd done, and though the principal had thanked her, she seemed to have forgotten to suggest Penelope for an award.

The final award, for a senior solo dance performance, went to the most popular girl in the school, Ellen Semorac. Her acceptance speech was drowned out by cheers and applause and she had to start over. Even though Penelope supposed that in some ways it might be a nice feeling to have your voice drowned out by cheers and applause, it still seemed a bit rude.

By the time it was Oscar and Penelope's turn, the crowd was getting Friday-afternoon fidgety. It wasn't the ideal time to do their presentation, but Penelope had promised Oscar that they would go up onstage together. If Penelope had been by herself in front of the whole assembly, she would have felt very anxious. But having Oscar right beside her (and knowing he was happy to do most of it) made her feel better. Her heartbeat was only slightly quicker than normal and her palms were only slightly sweatier. She leaned into the microphone.

"Introducing Oscar Finley with 'The Lucky Jar Rap,'" she said, and her voice was only a little bit wobbly. She moved away, and Oscar began immediately.

HE HELD BOTH HANDS IN THE AIR WITH HIS INDEX AND LITTLE FINGERS UP AND SWAYED FROM SIDE TO SIDE.

Hey there, homies, Chelsea Primary will go far

If we all remember our Luck-y Jars

Start with an empty and fill it to the top

Bring it to the fair so the crowd can shop, shop, SHOP.

THEN OSCAR TRIED TO DO THE MOONWALK.

Unfortunately, his moonwalk wasn't much better than his basketball. His shoes scraped and squeaked against the cement. But the girls in the senior class did not seem to care one bit. In fact, they started to clap. Their clapping accompanied the next verse. *It was very*

encouraging. So encouraging that Penelope decided (as a sacrifice for the good of the school) to join in the last verse.

We have a record to beat and this year's gonna rock
Stuff your jars with lollies, hey, stuff 'em with socks
Use your imagination, yeah, make 'em sublime
The main thing is to MAKE 'EM and get 'em here
ON TIME.

PENELOPE'S VOICE WAS A BIT WOBBLY, BUT THAT DIDN'T SEEM TO MATTER.

The cheers and applause were almost as loud as the cheers and applause that had drowned out Ellen Semorac's acceptance speech.

"That was a Very Good Idea, Oscar," Penelope whispered while everyone was still cheering.

"Well, you made a very good idea into a very good rap, Penny," he said.

Penelope glowed. She and Oscar were definitely a great team. She was also very happy with the second-last line. "Sublime" was an excellent word, and it had been entirely her idea.

The sock idea was Oscar's. Penelope wasn't quite as sure about that one.

Penelope *really* wanted to mention, while she still had the microphone, that the sock bit was definitely a joke and that no one should actually do it. But everyone was wandering off in a very Friday-afternoon manner, so she decided (after a while) to let that idea go.

"Have you ever, that you know about, had someone crushing on you?" Bob asked. The question was for everyone. Since camp, Rita and Tilly had started walking home with Penelope and Bob. Even though they only walked with her and Bob for (about) three hundred and fifty yards before they turned down a different street, sometimes Penelope wasn't so sure she liked this development.

Penelope had two main reasons for this. The first was that she loved spending time alone with Bob. Having a very best friend after *not* having a very best friend for a long time (well, forever) meant that Penelope wanted to take good care of their friendship.

The second reason was Rita Azul. Although *sometimes* Rita could be okay, most of the time she was mean. Penelope was not quite sure whether Rita was actually trying to be the meanest girl in the world or if it just came naturally, but either way, she was *VERY* good at it. In fact, every time Rita spoke, Penelope got a prickly sort of feeling. Like right now.

PENELOPE FELT THE PRICKLY FEELING GROWING.

"Well, *obviously* Penelope hasn't had anyone crushing on *her*," Rita said with a flip of her hand. "Like, *as if*."

Penelope felt a surge of ANGER, like the surge

STOP

that *used* to come before an outburst. But since she had (almost definitely) grown out of her outbursts, Penelope did not react. Now, when anyone (which usually meant Rita Azul) made a TERRIBLY RUDE comment, Penelope counted to three before she decided whether she was going to respond. This time, she decided not to. Responding to Rita sometimes made her even meaner.

Besides, although Penelope did not like or agree with Rita's TERRIBLY RUDE comment, she certainly, definitely didn't want anyone crushing on her. It looked exhausting to be crushed on, and possibly even a little bit dangerous.

Anyway (though Penelope suspected that Bob was itching to defend her), Rita didn't give anyone time to respond.

"I've got at least five boys crushing on me," she said in a high-pitched and showing-off way.

"Who would that be, Rita?" Tilly inter-jected. "I don't know anyone who has a crush on you." Since camp, Tilly was *interjecting* Rita more and more. Rita put her hands on her hips.

"No one any of you would know," she said. "They're all *older* boys from other schools."

"Like how old? And what other schools?" Bob asked. Rita's face flushed, then she looked down at the ground.

"I don't tell that kind of stuff," she said. "Telling is for babies."

Rita was always going on about how things were *for babies.* It was (one of) her not-very-nice qualities. Penelope had a strong suspicion that Rita wasn't telling the absolute truth about five older boys having a crush on her.

But really, she just wished everyone would stop talking about all that stuff. It was *very* distracting. Penelope was just glad that nobody had a crush on Bob—or on her!

"I'd like to sock that Rita Azul right on the nose," Bob said as soon as they were alone. For a moment, Penelope was worried that Bob's demonstration of socking Rita on the nose (using Penelope as a stand-in for Rita) might hurt. But Bob pulled her fist away from Penelope's nose (just) before it connected.

"Don't you even worry about her, Pen," Bob continued, barely taking a breath. "She is such a liar liar, pants on fire. I'll bet there's no one crushing on her at all. And it was so mean to say no one could possibly have a crush on you! Probably any boy in the whole wide world would like you."

Penelope felt her heart fill up. Bob was the best, best friend ever. As long as

Penelope had Bob by her side, she could cope with any mean thing Rita said.

"Thanks, Bob," Penelope replied. "But seriously, who would even want anyone to have a crush on them? Look at Alex and Joanna. He gets her in *headlocks*. I definitely would not like that one bit. I think crushes are silly."

The two of them walked along the footpath. Bob kicked a stone. It wasn't unusual for Bob to kick a stone, but it *was* unusual for her to be quiet. Penelope counted how many steps Bob was quiet for. Eight.

"Bob?" Penelope said finally. "Are you okay?"

Bob stopped walking. She sighed loudly. Then she sat on someone's low brick fence.

"Can I tell you something?" Bob asked. "Something you can't tell anybody, ever?"

It was entirely possible that sitting on a stranger's low brick fence was trespassing, but

STOP

Penelope took some deep breaths and tried to push that thought out of her mind so she could concentrate on what Bob wanted to tell her. This was just one of the things Penelope was willing to do as a very best friend. Though Bob wasn't a new very best friend anymore, Penelope still appreciated having someone to share special thoughts and secrets with. She would absolutely *die* before she betrayed Bob's trust. If that was absolutely necessary. Which it most probably wouldn't be.

"I pinkie promise," she said.

"Sometimes," Bob said, "I'm just thinking about totally normal stuff, and Tommy Stratton randomly pops into my head."

Penelope did not know what to say about that. She was used to things (like Pleasant Images) popping into her head randomly, but *not* thoughts about a *boy*.

"And this morning, I got a funny feeling here," Bob continued, putting her hand on her heart, "when I talked to him."

Penelope frowned. "What kind of a funny feeling?" she asked. As she asked, Penelope had a funny feeling of her own. It was a not-good funny feeling.

"IT'S SORT OF LIKE THINGS WENT NUTSO," BOB EXPLAINED WITH A GIGGLE.

"Like I'd swallowed a bug and it was spinning around inside me. Then I went all red in the face and after that I forgot where I was in my sentence and got tongue-tied and felt all *shy*."

"Oh," Penelope said, "that sounds awful." One of Bob's best talents was that she was not the tiniest bit shy.

"Well, that's the weirdest thing," Bob said. "It wasn't actually that bad at all."

On the low brick fence (where they were almost definitely trespassing), Penelope thought hard about what Bob was telling her. But thinking hard was not particularly helpful. It actually led to more questions.

Penelope cleared her throat. There was a question she had to ask. But she very much hoped the answer was no.

"Bob, do you think you have a crush on

Tommy Stratton?" Penelope asked. She tried to keep her voice normal when she mentioned his name. If Bob had a crush on him, it was possible she would start going very strange and getting into headlocks and things. It might even mean that Penelope and Bob would spend *less* time together. Penelope did not like that idea at all.

Tommy Stratton was quite a nice boy, but possibly the worst singer Penelope had ever heard. Unfortunately, Tommy didn't know that singing was *not* his talent.

He would be a very strange choice of person for Bob to get a crush on. Penelope crossed her fingers while she waited for the answer.

"I don't know, really," Bob giggled. "But wouldn't that be crazy? I mean, *Tommy Stratton!* I'll have to talk to him and see if it happens again."

Penelope frowned. She leaned into her very best friend.

"You've heard Tommy Stratton sing, right?" she asked.

"Yes," Bob squealed. "He's absolutely *rotten*!"

"Phew," Penelope said. "Because I heard love can make you blind. I was worried that it might have made you *deaf*."

Even though she hadn't actually said it to be funny (and she very much hoped Bob did *not* have a crush on Tommy Stratton and wouldn't start getting weird and headlocky), it was nice to make her very best friend crack up with laughter.

CHAPTER

Penelope struggled to set up her first-Saturday-of-the-month jewelry stall in front of her house. It was quite an effort, since it was *freezing* and very windy, plus she had a lot on her mind. Now that she'd had time to think about it, Penelope was pretty sure that if Bob did have a crush on Tommy Stratton, it would be Truly Terrible for their friendship.

She was also worried about whether she and Oscar would be able to break the Lucky

Jar record and make Penelope's dad *extremely* proud. But she was staying positive.

Unfortunately (most likely because it was freezing!), the street was quiet. The Coxley twins, Sam and Gus, were playing cricket in the middle of the road, but it was unlikely they would buy any of Penelope's jewelry.

In the distance, Penelope could see Doris from the Aged Care Center down the road, with her walking frame. Once a month, Penelope's class visited the Center to help entertain the elderly folk, so Penelope knew Doris quite well. In fact, Doris was probably her favorite elderly person (apart from Grandpa George and his friend Fred). As she came closer, Penelope could see that Doris had had a visit from the hairdresser. Her hair was a very interesting shade of purple, and curled very tight.

Penelope stood up as Doris arrived at the stall.

"Oh my," Doris said as she looked at Penelope's jewelry. "What lovely pieces. Did you make them all yourself, dear?"

Penelope smiled and nodded while Doris picked out the leather cord necklace with the lady-bird pendant she'd made out of modeling clay.

"You are so clever, young lady. I will cherish this," Doris said.

Her purse was hanging off the walking frame. Penelope helped her open it. Doris handed her a fifty-dollar bill. "Keep the change, dear," she said as she started back the way she had come.

It was an extremely generous gesture. Unfortunately, the fifty-dollar bill was Monopoly money. Penelope didn't say anything about that, though.

"Thanks, Doris," Penelope called out after her.

She took a deep breath. It was quite tough to part with her (second) favorite piece of jewelry. Monopoly money wasn't very useful in real life. On the *positive* side, though, Penelope was glad the ladybird had gone to someone who would cherish it. Just like she knew her dad would cherish the bow tie when she gave it to him (absolutely for free) next weekend.

But she decided to finish up the stall a bit earlier than usual.

As she came in the back door Penelope heard her mum talking on the phone in the kitchen. Penelope instantly knew who she was talking to. Her mum's voice changed tone when she spoke to Penelope's father. If tones had a shape, this one would be POINTY. Penelope stayed in the hallway. She knew it wasn't nice to snoop, but somehow she couldn't help listening in.

"Okay, you can take the kids for the weekend, Tony," Penelope's mum said. "I'll be at the fair anyway—I'm running one of the stalls. But I'll help Harry pack before I go. Penelope will want to organize herself."

There was a pause as Penelope's dad spoke. Then came her mum's voice again.

"Oh, for God's sake, Tony, why would you put that idea in her head? I will not take her to the doctor. Being a little bit on the small side is not an illness."

Penelope rolled her eyes. SOMETIMES HER MUM WAS INCREDIBLY STUBBORN!

There was another pause while her dad

talked. Now Penelope could actually hear him through the other end of the phone, though she couldn't make out what he was saying.

"Just don't you disappoint them, Tony. They're both really looking forward to next weekend. If you let them down again, I swear I'll—"

Penelope's mum didn't finish her sentence. Penelope supposed that was because her dad had hung up. That had happened before.

Suddenly, Penelope felt very annoyed and frustrated and Not Positive At All. It could have had something to do with Bob (maybe) having a crush on Tommy Stratton. It could have had something to do with Monopoly money.

But mostly, it had to do with her mum being pointy to her dad. Sometimes, Penelope wondered if her dad had left because her mum was pointy to him. Penelope never (even when she felt Extremely Grumpy) talked to her dad like that. She would NEVER EVER take the risk. He might disappear altogether.

She stomped into the kitchen.

"Hi, Poss," her mum said (as though nothing bad had just happened). "How did your jewelry stall go?"

"TERRIBLE," Penelope said huffily. She put her hands on her hips. "What percentile am I in?" she demanded. (Penelope had googled percentiles. She still didn't quite understand what they were, but she knew it was something to do with measuring sizes.)

Penelope's mum frowned.

"I don't know, Penelope," she said. "But I do know that I was small when I was your age. And I do know that there's nothing wrong with that."

"So," Penelope continued, "you don't even know my percentile." She paused and narrowed her eyes. "Dad knows Sienna's percentile. But that's probably because he cares about her. That's how things are in his *new* family."

She shook her head, feeling the words sting even as she said them. "Not like here," she finished.

PENELOPE'S WORDS WERE LIKE BULLETS.

When they hit, her mother's mouth fell open and there were (possibly, it was hard to be sure) tears in her eyes.

It was all a bit of a shock. Part of Penelope wanted to run up to her mum and hug her. Penelope's mum hardly ever cried. Penelope had certainly never made her cry before (that she knew of). She felt awful, but in a strange way, kind of powerful.

It was actually quite satisfying to slam the door on her way out.

Penelope lay on her bed wishing her mum would come in. Now, she didn't feel powerful at all. She just felt mean. And sorry. And she wanted a tight hug. If it were possible to rub out words (like you did if you made a mistake with a drawing), Penelope would have done so in a heartbeat. She squeezed blue teddy hard, which was helpful, but she still found herself looking at the door, wishing it would open.

It was like a miracle when it did. Penelope jumped out of bed, ran over to her mum, and hugged her around the waist. It had been a long time since her mum had picked her up, and (even though Penelope was very small for her age) her mum practically toppled over as she carried Penelope to her bed.

She had something with her. It was a booklet with a plastic cover. On the plastic cover, it said *CHILD HEALTH RECORD, Penelope Kingston*.

"Poss," her mum said, fluffing a pillow and leaning back with Penelope snuggled beside her. "I don't think it matters because you're absolutely perfect the way you are. But this booklet will tell you what percentile you were on when you were Sienna's age."

Penelope's mum opened the booklet to the tab that said *3½ year visit*. Penelope could see that she had been in the fortieth percentile, which meant that she had been a bit below the average height, even then. Then her mum flipped over to a different page. There, stuck in quite randomly, was a photo of Penelope at about 3½ years old. **Even though she knew she probably shouldn't think this about herself, Penelope thought she looked very cute.** She was wearing leopard-print leggings and a denim shirt and smiling a very happy smile. She definitely looked like she was cared for.

Penelope leaned into her mum and tucked her head on her shoulder.

"I'm sorry," she whispered.

Penelope's mum kissed the top of her head.

"I know," she said. "It's okay."

Penelope breathed in.

"I was cute," she said.

"You were adorable," her mum agreed.

Penelope knew that photo must have been taken only months before her parents split up.

"Then how could Dad leave?" she asked.

Her mum hugged her tight.

"Poss, it didn't have anything to do with you," she said. "It wasn't about you and it wasn't about Harry. It was about him and me. We just weren't a good match."

"That's not a great answer," Penelope told her mum in a teasing voice.

"It's all I've got, kid," her mum replied.

"But I was adorable?" Penelope just had to hear it one more time.

Her mum released her from the hug and smiled.

Penelope smiled back. She still didn't really understand why her dad left them. **But she absolutely knew her mum loved her.**

She thought it was likely that Harry did too, though he would never say anything like that out loud.

"You still are," her mum said with a wink. "Some of the time!"

CHAPTER

5

Normally, on a Monday morning, Penelope felt alert, refreshed and ready for a brand-new school week. Today, though, she felt tired and floppy. Seeing Bob made her feel a bit better. Well, it did until (before she had even asked to see the Lucky Jars Penelope had made over the weekend!) Bob whispered in her ear.

"Okay, I'm going to talk to Tommy and you tell me how I look." PENELOPE TRIED NOT

TO FROWN. If Bob had a crush on Tommy, Penelope would probably have to talk her out of it. There was no way she could tolerate Bob getting all headlocky with Tommy. But there was still a chance that Bob was mistaken, so there was probably no point saying anything just yet.

She watched as Bob crossed the courtyard to where Tommy Stratton was playing handball against the free wall with Felix Unger. He was a lot better at handball than he was at singing. The ball flew backward and forward between the boys until Bob tapped Tommy on the shoulder. Tommy turned around and missed the next shot altogether. As Felix chased the ball across the courtyard, Penelope focused hard on Bob and Tommy.

Though Penelope couldn't hear what they were saying, it was clear that Bob was not being her normal self. For starters, she didn't normally throw her head back when she laughed, like she was doing now. She was also quite red in the face. And after she'd finished talking to Tommy she walked backward into a pole in a way that looked very clumsy and un-Bob-like. It was *not* a good sign. In fact (and this was very weird but true), watching Bob behave like that made Penelope feel quite achy in the bones.

"Oh my God," Bob said breathlessly when she reached Penelope. "Tommy is the cutest boy ever! I've definitely got a crush!"

As far as Penelope was concerned, Tommy Stratton wasn't even *close* to being the cutest boy in the world. She put down her school bag carefully (remembering the Lucky Jars inside) and sat down on the bench seat in the courtyard.

Really, this was the time to talk Bob out of having a crush altogether. But somehow, Penelope didn't feel the strength to even *object*. She just felt teary and weak (and this was terrible, because crying at school was incredibly embarrassing and almost as bad as having an outburst). Bob sat down next to her.

"Hey, are you okay, Pen?" she asked. "You look kind of pale." Penelope blinked back a tear.

She was about to mention her worry about Bob spending all her time with Tommy (and away from her) when the bell rang.

Class that morning was very busy. There was reading time and then Penelope did some research for her assignment on her chosen endangered species (*Burramys parvus*—the mountain pygmy possum). Penelope was very passionate about this project, but today, the information wasn't sinking in. Penelope's head felt thick and foggy. Even Joanna (the naughtiest girl in the class) had written more than Penelope. Actually, Penelope felt like everything was moving slower than usual today.

It wasn't until after recess that Penelope got to show Ms. Pike her Lucky Jars.

"Oh, Penelope," Ms. Pike said as Penelope arranged her Lucky Jars on the teacher's desk, where they could inspire other kids to bring in their own. "These are truly delightful. I can't even tell what they were originally for, they're decorated so prettily."

Each of Penelope's four Lucky Jars was covered with cloth over the lid, held down by an elastic band. As a special creative touch, she had used spotty toweling from  one of the jumpsuits her mum had kept from when she was a baby. The spotty toweling looked **great** with all the colors of the sweets inside.

Ms. Pike was a lovely teacher and at any other time, her praise would have made Penelope feel warm inside. But, oddly, she actually felt kind of cold.

Oscar walked up behind her  and put his Lucky Jars next to Penelope's. Though they definitely weren't as pretty as Penelope's, he'd done quite a good job. Oscar's lids were all black (Penelope suspected he'd colored them in with a perma-nent marker) with a white skull and cross-bones (Wite-Out).

Although she detected that there were fart bombs in among the sweets, and Penelope felt like telling Oscar to remove them, for some reason, she couldn't be bothered mentioning it. There were only three other jars on Ms. Pike's desk so far (and all three looked suspiciously like someone had been taking things out of them, rather than putting things in), but Penelope did not comment. She just stared at them until they went fuzzy in front of her eyes. She felt very weird.

"Penelope," Ms. Pike said, "I don't think you're well." She put her hand on Penelope's forehead. "Oh, you poor thing," she said soothingly, "you're all clammy."

Ms. Pike looked around the classroom.

"Bob," she said, "could you take Penelope to the nurse, please?"

Penelope was hardly ever sick enough to miss school, but the next day—even though she really wanted to be there to help inspire kids to bring their Lucky Jars and to double-check whether Bob was going to get weird now that she had a crush on Tommy Stratton—there was no way she could make it. Having the flu was like having a cold, but multiplied by ten. One minute Penelope was on fire, and the next minute she felt as though icicles were being pressed into her.

Penelope's mum had to work that day and the next, so she dropped Penelope (in her pajamas, dressing gown, and slippers and with an overnight bag with blue teddy on the top) off at Grandpa George's.

If Penelope absolutely *had* to be sick, it

was best to be sick at her grandpa's house. Grandpa George tucked Penelope into the big bed in the spare room and, without Penelope even having to ask, snuggled blue teddy in with her.

Penelope drifted in and out of sleep. Some of the drifting was quite nice. A bit like Pleasant Images, but sleepier. At one stage, she and Oscar were back at assembly doing the Lucky Jar rap. It was similar to the real experience except that Penelope was wearing a beautiful pink gown, and Oscar was in a suit.

One bit of drifting, though, was NOT NICE AT ALL. In this, Penelope was surrounded by a circle of girls who were, somehow, all Rita Azul. Through the gap between two of the Rita Azuls, Penelope could see Bob across the oval in the distance. She called out to her very best friend. Penelope held her breath as Bob started running toward her. Then (RIGHT IN THE MIDDLE OF PENELOPE'S DRIFT, WHERE HE CERTAINLY WASN'T WELCOME!) Tommy Stratton appeared. And instead of rescuing Penelope, Bob flew into Tommy's arms.

That drift was extremely upsetting. Fortunately it was cut off by Grandpa's voice as he recited poems while sitting in the chair beside her bed.

Penelope didn't really understand much about the poems he recited, but she didn't care. There was something soothing about a tiger burning bright and mermaids singing, though she wasn't sure why. It was just nice to hear his voice.

By the following day, Penelope felt well enough to get out of bed and go into Grandpa George's living room.

Normally, Penelope liked things that matched, but she adored Grandpa George's chaotic living room because it matched *him*. She liked his giant desk with the purple fringed lamp and she liked the glass cabinet that held fourteen very unusual teapots (her favorite was the Angelfish, where the spout was the fish's mouth). But what she *adored* most about Grandpa George's living room was the ceiling. It was covered with stars, like in a planetarium, and, at this time in the afternoon, just as it was getting dark, the stars started to glow.

Penelope lay back on the red velvet couch and Grandpa covered her with a mohair rug. Though she wasn't going hot and cold anymore, Penelope was extremely snotty. Grandpa put a fresh box of tissues next to her and lay back on the green couch opposite.

BOTH OF THEM LOOKED UP AT THE INDOOR SKY.

"Your mum's picking you up at seven," he said, "straight after the fair meeting."

Penelope nodded. This year, her mum was in charge of the craft stall, which was selling her jewelry, as well as other things.

"And she had to do a bit of wrangling, but she managed to get the day off work tomorrow to look after you at home."

Penelope blew her nose. It was the type of

gurgly nose blow that could have been extremely embarrassing, but it didn't really matter in front of Grandpa George.

"I HAVE to be better before the weekend," Penelope said in a cloggy voice. Penelope knew that her snotty nose and cloggy voice meant she would have to stay home again tomorrow. Which meant that the *earliest* she would be well again and back at school was Friday. That was cutting it pretty fine to make sure the Lucky Jars were under control. The idea of not being well by the weekend was unthinkable!

"You know, Dad's coming over for the fair"—unfortunately Penelope snorted mid-sentence, but then she soldiered on—"and Harry's soccer match. It's going to be just the three of us, and we're going to stay at a *fancy* hotel."

Penelope must have been getting at least a

little bit better, because she was able to conjure up several different Pleasant Images of hotel rooms.

"If I'm not better by the time Dad arrives, I'll absolutely *die*," she said dramatically.

Penelope looked sideways at her grandpa to check that he understood how serious the situation was. Though he was still looking up at the stars, she could detect a slight frown. But he didn't say anything.

"If I'm not better by the time Dad arrives, I'll absolutely *DIE*," Penelope repeated, in case he didn't hear her properly the first time.

Grandpa George still didn't answer.

Sometimes, Grandpa George didn't hear too well, but Penelope was fairly sure he *had* heard her. It seemed to Penelope that Grandpa's hearing got worse when her dad was mentioned. He never said anything bad about Penelope's father, but sometimes Penelope got the feeling that he wasn't Grandpa George's favorite person. Grandpa George was her mum's dad, so Penelope supposed that he had to be on her side.

When he spoke, he was his usual gentle self. "I'm sure you'll be all better by the weekend," he said softly. "And I truly hope you have a lovely time with your father, sweetheart." He opened his mouth, like he was about to say something else, but then closed it again. (Sometimes he could be very like Harry, thought Penelope—though clearly Grandpa was a lot wiser.) "Shall we consult your chart?"

Penelope sat up a little. It was always a treat to have Grandpa consult her chart. Being a Gemini (the twins) was tricky. Sometimes Penelope felt like she had two different people inside her. It was one of the reasons why Penelope used to have outbursts (before she almost definitely grew out of them). Grandpa's charts *could* be confusing, like the poetry he read to her yesterday. But usually (if she could figure out what it meant), they gave her some good advice.

Penelope waited while her Grandpa rustled around in his desk.

Finally, he came back with a printout. He sat at the end of Penelope's couch and lifted her feet onto his lap. He gave them a quick rub, then began reading aloud.

"'Communication is important this week. Sometimes the truth needs to be spoken, even when it's unpleasant.'"

Grandpa paused. "Hmmm, that's interesting," he said. "Is there anything going on in your life that this might relate to?"

Penelope thought hard.

Perhaps the truth that needed to be spoken was about Bob and her silly crush on Tommy Stratton? Now that Penelope was starting to feel better, she *did* think she might be able to talk Bob out of it.

In fact (since the truth had to be spoken, even if it was unpleasant), she already had some very good points to help Bob see things *her* way.

CHAPTER

6

By Thursday, Penelope didn't feel nearly as sick. But her nose was runny in a way that would have been difficult (and embarrassing) to deal with at school, so she stayed home with her mum.

Penelope had to put away Harry's soccer cleats (which he had left right in the middle of the floor) and his dirty jersey (flung over the back of the couch) and pack away her mum's card game (floor and couch) before she could relax in the lounge room. But, after that, Penelope and her mum curled up on the couch and watched an old movie.

Straight after the movie there was an advertisement for a GIANT bra. It was the sort of GIANT bra that no child should have to look at while having a sick day, so Penelope switched channels.

And there he was. On TV. Penelope's father.

Even though it had been happening quite a lot lately, it always came as a surprise for Penelope to see him on TV. Penelope fought the urge to walk right up to the screen and wave.

It was very strange to think that he was right there in the lounge room with her (and her mum) and yet not there at all. Her dad certainly looked important in his navy suit and yellow tie.

From the side view, when the cameras changed angles, his nose was just a little bit pointy like Penelope's. Penelope

leaned forward on the couch and cupped her chin in her hands.

"These are *core* promises," her dad said in a very clear voice. "They are blueprints for our nation. Improved transport. Better health care. The education our children deserve. If you vote for us, you vote for greatness."

When another politician came on-screen, Penelope muted the TV.

"Dad is going to improve transport, and health care, and education," she told her mum (in case she hadn't been listening properly). **Truly, her dad was so inspiring.**

Penelope thought that if she and Oscar had been even a tenth as inspiring as her dad was, they could get kids to make Lucky Jars. It hadn't been looking good before she got sick, though. She would have to wait until tomorrow to see.

"Well," said her mum, "he's certainly a good talker." She paused, then reached for Penelope's hand. "I'm sure Tony will do his best to keep those promises. I'm sure that he *wants* to improve transport and health care and education," she said. "But actions speak louder than words. It's not easy to achieve all those things."

Penelope barely heard her mum speak because she was so *inspired* by her dad. She blew her nose. It actually felt quite clear now. In fact, she felt quite well.

The thing was (though she wouldn't say it

aloud to her mum) Penelope thought she was quite like her father.

He was very good at convincing people to see things his way. When he wrote speeches, he would note bullet points on an index card, to remind him of what to say. That way, he wasn't just reading out a speech. It sounded more natural, and it meant he could have eye contact with his audience.

Perhaps it was too late to inspire kids to make more Lucky Jars. But she was absolutely (well, almost completely) sure that she could convince Bob not to have a crush on Tommy Stratton. Truly, it was probably her *duty* to get Bob thinking clearly again, just like it was her dad's duty to improve transport and health care and education.

After all: *Sometimes the truth needs to be spoken, even when it's unpleasant.*

Suddenly, Penelope felt well enough to get started on her bullet points right away.

REASONS FOR BOB NOT TO HAVE A CRUSH ON TOMMY STRATTON
- Tommy is DEFINITELY not the cutest boy alive.
- He has the worst singing voice EVER.
- Kids with crushes get silly (and headlocky).
- Having a crush could mean spending less time with your very best friend. ✿ ✿ ✿

Penelope felt perfectly well on Friday morning. She was a bit nervous about telling Bob the (unpleasant) truth about her crush on Tommy Stratton, but the index card Penelope held in her hand was reassuring. She got to school early so she could practice her speech.

Finally, Bob appeared at the school gate. She squealed when she saw Penelope, and ran over to the bench seat to greet her.

"How *are* you, Pen?" Bob asked, sitting down next to Penelope with a thud. "Ms. Pike told us you had the flu. Hooly dooly, I've missed you!"

Penelope breathed deeply. **Bob was the very best sort of best friend.** Suddenly, Penelope had second thoughts about giving her speech. But then she checked herself. It was *because* Bob was the very best sort of best friend that Penelope had to go ahead with this. She absolutely could NOT lose her to Tommy Stratton!

"I had a rough couple of days," Penelope told Bob. "But I also had some time to think." Penelope tilted her head to the side and checked her bullet points.

"Bob, I don't think you should have a crush on Tommy Stratton," she said.

Bob wrinkled her eyebrows.

"What are you talking about, Pen?" she asked.

Penelope sighed. It was time for the unpleasant truths.

"For starters, he's not actually the cutest boy in the world," she said.

"Well, he is to me," Bob said. "And of course you don't think he is, because *YOU* don't have a crush on him."

"And he has a terrible singing voice," Penelope reminded Bob.

"Well, I won't ask him to sing to me," Bob replied.

Penelope exhaled loudly. Bob could be very stubborn. She checked her next bullet point.

"Kids with crushes get silly," she appealed.

"And having a crush on Tommy might mean that you spend less time with me!"

Penelope hadn't meant to blurt those last two points out like that, altogether. But perhaps it wasn't such a bad thing to do. Because just then, Bob pinched Penelope on the thigh (in a good way). Then she bumped Penelope with her shoulder.

"So's, Pen. I *have* got a crush on Tommy," she said. "I'm not going to stop. But I'm not going to ditch *you*, either."

Penelope looked at her bullet points. Honestly, they hadn't been that helpful.

"Are you still going to be my best friend, Bob?" she asked nervously.

"Of course I will. Don't be nutso! I'll be your BFF forever," Bob said, nudging her again.

Penelope felt a small smile forming inside her.

"Are you going to let Tommy get you in headlocks and pull you around in circles?" she asked. "I'm not sure I could watch that."

"No way, José," Bob said. "Not going to happen."

Penelope felt the smile grow into a giggle. Bob was just so—well, she was just Bob. And, even though Penelope wished her speech had changed Bob's mind about Tommy, Penelope wouldn't change a thing about her (very) best friend.

"Come on, Pen," Bob said. "There's something you have to see!"

Bob led Penelope into the classroom. Although she did stop briefly at Tommy Stratton's table (twelve seconds—just talking, no headlocks), Penelope was patient.

"Welcome back, Penelope!" Ms. Pike said,

standing in front of her desk. "How about a round of applause for Oscar and Penelope, please, class?"

Penelope wound her way through the tables to the front of the room, surprised by the applause. She'd only missed three days of school. Then again, she was almost *never* sick.

Oscar Finley joined her up the front. When Ms. Pike stepped away from her desk, Penelope gasped.

THERE WAS NOT A SPARE INCH ON MS. PIKE'S DESK. IT WAS *COVERED* IN LUCKY JARS.

There were big ones and small ones. They were bright and colorful, and there were LOADS of them—Penelope counted approximately forty-three jars.

But then Ms. Pike opened the cabinet behind her desk, and Penelope could see at least twelve more in there.

"It's the best response we've ever had," Ms. Pike said. "Congratulations."

"We're bound to break the Lucky Jar record!" Oscar said, breaking into the Lucky Jar rap in front of the whole class.

This time (though it was quite hard to rap when she absolutely could not stop grinning from ear to ear), Penelope joined in from the first verse. She even managed a (not too bad) moonwalk.

Perhaps she hadn't been able to convince Bob not to have a crush. But obviously, she still had *some* of her dad's skill when it came to inspiring people.

If they managed to sell them all, her dad was going to be SO PROUD! And there was only one more sleep before the fair!

CHAPTER

7

Penelope's dad was due to arrive at nine a.m. on Saturday. Penelope woke at seven thirty a.m. to the soothing strums of the harp alarm on her iPhone. She showered and got dressed in her favorite jeans, T-shirt, and sandals. She double-checked her overnight bag to make sure she had everything she would need for the fair, a sleepover at a *fancy* hotel, and Harry's soccer match tomorrow. Then she took the bow-tie badge from her jewelry stand, ready to give it to her dad, and did a super-duper tidy of her bedroom, just in case he would see it.

Since she knew she would most likely be eating from the top of the food pyramid ("eat rarely") that day, she decided to kick-start the day with some high-fiber cereal.

While Penelope was eating her cereal, her mum rushed into the kitchen carrying Penelope's jewelry stand (minus the bow-tie badge). Penelope would have liked to point out that her mum's odd socks were quite visible under her jeans (one white with red flowers and one bright green with yellow stripes), but there was no time for her to change anyway.

"Hey, Poss," Penelope's mum said, "I've got to fly. I've got some setting up to do for the craft stall. Have you seen my car keys?"

Penelope struggled to shake off

the feeling that she really should be going with her mum to help set up the craft stall and to make sure the Lucky Jars were nicely displayed. But it was even more important to be here when her dad arrived so they could start the weekend the right way.

Penelope pointed to a hook on the kitchen wall where she'd put the car keys after finding them in the pantry.

"Ah, you're a legend," her mum said, picking up the keys. She gave Penelope a hug. It was quite a long, squeezy hug, and Penelope had to remind her mum that she was running late. When she got to the front door, Penelope's mum turned around.

"I'll see you there," she said. "I hope you have a good time with your father."

"Of course I will," Penelope replied. "It's going to be the best weekend ever."

It was a bit annoying that her mum kept standing at the door. She was letting a draft in and making herself even later.

"Call me if you need anything," she said, finally turning to go. "I'll make sure I have my phone close by."

Penelope shrugged. If she needed anything, her *dad* could take care of it.

It was *not* easy trying to get Harry up early on a Saturday morning. Penelope had to use her old trick of pulling the duvet right off her brother and leaving it far enough from the bed that he would have to get up to put it back.

Unfortunately, just like their mum, who had packed for him, Harry was not good at being organized, so Penelope checked his overnight bag while he took care of his soccer gear. By 8:56 a.m. (four minutes before their dad was due to arrive!), Harry still hadn't cleaned his teeth. When he started playing a game on the Xbox, Penelope took ten very deep breaths, but she didn't comment. It was Extremely Important that she and Harry weren't arguing when their dad arrived. They needed to impress him with their good manners.

Penelope waited near the front door with their overnight bags.

At 8:59 a.m., there was a knock. Their father was right on time.

Penelope smiled her brightest smile and opened the door.

Penelope had seen this on several TV shows (even with girls who were bigger than her).

STRAIGHT AFTER
SHE OPENED THE
DOOR, SHE LEAPED
INTO HER FATHER'S
ARMS.

He was
carrying
a briefcase,
and it was a little
awkward when
it got lodged between
them, but (other
than that) it was a
successful move.

"Well, well, well," he said as he put Penelope
back on the carpet in the hall. One of her legs
landed more heavily than the other, but she
corrected herself very quickly. "It's great to see
you. You look terrific."

"Thanks," Penelope said.

Her dad was dressed in a gray suit with a navy tie. It was the kind of thing he wore to work. **Penelope was pleased that he also thought this weekend was Very Important.** Penelope almost wished she'd put on her best dress too, but that wouldn't be very practical for going on rides at the fair.

Penelope closed the door and followed her dad into the lounge room. As they came in, Harry pressed pause on his game. For Harry, that was Very Polite.

"Hi, Dad," he said.

"Hi, mate," their dad said. He ruffled Harry's hair (without saying anything about a haircut), and Harry let him. **So far, things were going PERFECTLY.**

Penelope felt very happy to see her dad and Harry sitting side by side on the couch, playing Xbox together. She was pleasantly surprised to discover that they made similar sounds (*oohs*, *aahs*, and grunts) as they played. Penelope had never really thought her dad and Harry were similar at all, and she definitely wanted them to have something in common. Having things in common was a Very Good Thing for strong family ties (especially the stretchy kind).

Penelope sat on the armchair next to the couch, listening. Harry was getting quite chatty. In between the *oohs* and *aahs* and grunts, Harry and their dad discussed strategies to help Harry's soccer team win the game on Sunday. At one point, Harry even raced upstairs and brought down his soccer jersey (number sixteen) to show their dad.

Although Penelope was conscious that they should get going soon, she was Very Patient as she sat in her armchair. In fact, she was quite sure her father was going to point out how patient Penelope was being any second now.

Or minute.

Finally, her dad stood up.

"So, sweetheart," he said, "is there something you'd like to show me?"

Penelope flew up the stairs. (Not literally. Literally, it was more like a power walk.) There were loads of things she wanted to show her dad. Not to mention the special gift she had for him! It was a good feeling to see him nodding his head in approval as he looked around.

"It's very neat, Penelope," he said with a smile. "You get that from me."

Penelope felt like she was glowing from the inside out. She angled her head toward a particular wall. Just as she'd hoped, her father's eyes rested on the award certificates that were pinned up there in perfect rows.

"I'm actually the number one award-winner in my whole school," Penelope told her father.

IT WAS EXTREMELY SATISFYING TO SEE HIS REACTION.

"Well, that is terrific," he said, patting Penelope's shoulder. "Good work." As he took his hand away, her dad checked his watch.

Penelope was (just a tiny bit) worried that

she was losing his attention. But it was only a tiny worry. She knew she had something that would definitely get it back.

"Close your eyes, Dad," she said.

Her dad closed his eyes. Penelope opened her dresser drawer and took out the bow-tie badge she'd made.

"Open."

He opened his eyes and inspected the badge in Penelope's hand.

"Well, well, well," he said. Penelope thought maybe he was too overwhelmed to speak. "A bow tie. Is that for me?"

Penelope nodded.

"I made it," she said.

"Thank you, sweetheart," her dad said. "It's terrific."

Penelope stood on her dressing-table stool

and pinned the badge to the lapel of her dad's suit.

"Very smart," her dad said, looking in Penelope's mirror.

"You'll be able to see all the rest of my jewelry in the craft stall at the fair," Penelope told him. She paused. "I'm not sure they'll sell very quickly," she said *modestly*, "but we'd better get going just in case."

Penelope's dad tapped his watch this time. Inside Penelope was a weird, fluttery, not very *positive* feeling that she couldn't explain.

"Actually, sweetheart," he said. "That reminds me. Something's come up."

CHAPTER

8

It's going to be all right, Penelope told herself once with each stair (twelve tellings in total) on the way back down to the lounge room.

When they got there, Penelope's dad sat on the (single-person-all-by-himself) armchair and Penelope sat on the couch next to her brother. For some reason, their dad parted the curtains behind his chair and looked out the window before he spoke.

"It's been great seeing you guys," he said.

Penelope frowned. The fluttery, anxious feeling was drowning out her *It's going to be all right* chant. Harry fidgeted with his soccer jersey. Their father cleared his throat.

"It's unfortunate, but something has come up for work and I need to fly home straightaway. As a politician, sometimes I have to sacrifice personal pleasures in the name of the public. It's a commitment I make . . ."

He kept talking, but Penelope couldn't pay attention.

Harry stood up and his soccer jersey fell to the carpet. Penelope watched as her brother walked over to the window and pulled the curtains apart. Penelope saw a car and driver parked right outside their house. Harry shook his head at Penelope. Then he blew out a sigh and rolled his eyes.

Straightaway, Penelope realized that the

car and driver were waiting to take their dad to the airport. Sometimes, Penelope wished she wasn't so good at deducing (most) things, because that meant their dad had known about this the whole time he had been here.

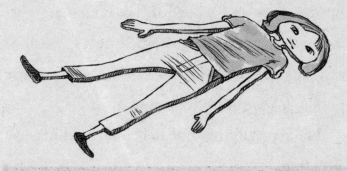

THE THOUGHT MADE PENELOPE FEEL AS FLAT AS A PANCAKE.

"What I *will* say," their dad continued, reaching into the breast pocket of his suit, "is that I've kept the reservation at the hotel for you two and your mother. You'll still have a great weekend, with the fair today and the soccer match . . ."

"Blah, blah, blah," Harry said, walking back from the window.

Penelope tried to gather up her flat-as-a-pancake feelings. Part of her wanted to jump up and slap a hand over Harry's mouth. His behavior was definitely NOT GOOD for stretchy family ties. But being flat as a pancake, she couldn't quite find enough spring to even get up off the couch.

"I beg your pardon, Harry?" their father said.

Harry narrowed his eyes. "So you're going to ditch us again. Big deal. It's not like we're not used to it," Harry said.

"Now, that's uncalled-for," their dad said. He opened his wallet and put some money down on the coffee table.

"Whatever, Dad," Harry said, shrugging as though he didn't care. But Penelope knew that he DID care. She could tell by the way he tapped his foot against the carpet, like he always did when he was excited or agitated.

For a moment, Penelope felt worse for Harry than she did for herself. Harry had really tried this time.

"Come on, Penelope," Harry said in a defeated voice. "Let's go and get ready for the fair."

Harry had not held Penelope's hand for a Very Long Time, but he kept doing it all the way up the stairs, and all the way to her bedroom. Perhaps it was the way Harry was looking after her that started pumping Penelope up from feeling flat as a pancake.

There were a lot of things Penelope had tried not to remember. On the stairs (third to seventh), she remembered how their dad had canceled a holiday the day before they were supposed to go. Then, just a couple of weeks later, he'd sent photos of his *NEW* family on holiday in Hawaii. (Penelope had never been anywhere like that in her *ENTIRE* life.) At the time, she didn't even let herself get angry (well, not at her dad anyway, though she did have a couple of outbursts at home).

From stairs seven to twelve, she remembered how Sienna had been allowed to eat bubblegum ice cream right before dinnertime. Halfway down the hall, she remembered how happy he had seemed about Sienna being on the seventieth percentile.

Just because Sienna was bigger than Penelope had been at that age, that didn't mean she was better (or that she should be allowed bubblegum ice cream right before dinner). That thought pumped Penelope right back to her usual size. She was Very Aware that she should try to stop thinking like that. She had a terrible feeling that if she got pumped up too much, she might just POP. There was no way she could have an outburst at her dad. That would be the very worst thing EVER for stretchy family ties.

But by the time she got to her room, Penelope couldn't help thinking about the way her dad had smiled as he corrected Sienna when she kept missing out on the five and the eight.

"Guys," her dad called up the stairs, "I have to go now."

Now, instead of feeling flat as a pancake, Penelope felt like she was being blown up like a balloon. Her temples throbbed and the palms of her hands felt sweaty.

"Wait," she called.

Since her dad was standing right at the

THEN SHE (PRACTICALLY) BOUNCED DOWN THE STAIRS.

bottom, Penelope nearly thwacked into him.
And then it happened.

Penelope *POPPED*.

"THIS IS ABSOLUTELY NOT FAIR,
DAD! DON'T YOU EVEN UNDERSTAND HOW
DISAPPOINTING THIS IS FOR ME AND
HARRY?"

"Calm down, sweetheart," her dad said. "I really hoped this weekend would work out as planned. But I'm a busy man. Sometimes work gets in the way."

"BUT YOU PROMISED!" Penelope yelled.

Penelope's dad put his hand on her shoulder. "Come on, Penelope," he said in a soothing voice. "That's not exactly true. I didn't actually *promise* anything."

Now Penelope felt angrier than ever. Her dad had never (not since he left them anyway) seen Penelope have an outburst. She suspected that he might be a bit shocked by the way her face had gone red and her veins were popping out. But she couldn't stop it now. The words were tumbling out all by themselves.

"WELL, YOU DID PROMISE!" she screamed. "MAYBE NOT IN WORDS, BUT YOU DID PROMISE."

A car horn beeped outside. Penelope ignored it.

"HARRY IS IN HIS FIRST GRAND FINAL EVER. DO YOU EVEN KNOW HOW GOOD HE IS?"

She paused. Now that she'd started, she couldn't stop. But there were so many things to be angry about, she had to choose.

"I BET YOU WOULDN'T DO THIS TO YOUR NEW FAMILY," she yelled. "I BET YOU WOULD NEVER DISAP- POINT SIENNA."

Now she was on a roll—nothing could stop her. She barreled on, drowning out the long hoot of the car horn outside.

"OBVIOUSLY YOU CARE ABOUT YOUR NEW FAMILY MORE THAN US. BUT YOU KNOW WHAT? SIENNA ISN'T PER- FECT. SHE CAN'T EVEN COUNT TO TEN

PROPERLY. SHE KEEPS MISSING OUT ON THE FIVE AND EIGHT."

She paused for a moment to let that sink in.

"AND I'LL HAVE THAT BADGE BACK, THANK YOU," she finished.

As her dad unpinned the badge, Penelope looked up to the landing. Harry was leaning over the banister with his hand over his mouth, looking very surprised.

"That is no way to behave, Penelope Kingston," her dad said firmly. "You know I have a big job and that I have to make sacrifices sometimes. It's just the way it is."

"WELL, THE WAY IT IS SUCKS," Penelope said. "AND IF YOU CAN'T ADMIT THAT, YOU'RE ONLY CHEATING YOURSELF."

Penelope's dad shook his head, as though he couldn't quite believe what he was hearing.

"I can't enter into a debate about this at the moment," he said. "We'll talk about this later."

Then Penelope's father turned and walked out the front door.

"Hey," Harry called down from the landing. "Go you! You sure told him."

Penelope was silent.

"Penelope?"

She put her head in her hands and listened as Harry came down the stairs (three at a time, with big thumps). Outbursts were always exhausting, but this had been her worst outburst EVER.

"Hey, sis," Harry said, "you just told the truth." He paused for a second. "Even if it isn't nice, it *is* the truth," he continued. "The way it is *does* suck."

Penelope thought about the advice from Grandpa's chart.

Communication is important this week. Sometimes the truth needs to be spoken, even when it's unpleasant.

Perhaps the chart was totally wrong this time. She had told Bob the unpleasant truth about her crush on Tommy Stratton, and that hadn't worked. Luckily Bob had been okay about Penelope's speech.

But this? With her dad?

Maybe family ties couldn't be stretched that far. Maybe she'd just gone and broken them completely.

SNAP.

CHAPTER

9

The fair was buzzing by the time Penelope and Harry arrived. The sun was shining and there was a gentle breeze. Even though her morning had been EXTREMELY difficult, Penelope couldn't help but feel the excitement all around her.

The basketball court had been (really and not just in Penelope's imagination) completely transformed. It was covered with stalls, and there were people everywhere. Even though her shift on the Lucky Jar stall wasn't until one thirty p.m., Penelope led Harry straight there. Gwen, from the Parents Committee, was looking after it.

There were no Lucky Jar customers just at that moment, but Penelope was still tempted to help out. The jars weren't spaced very evenly— she would start by fixing that. She was just taking her backpack off when Bob ran up and stopped her.

"Oh no, you don't, Penny Kingston," Bob squealed. "I've been waiting *FOREVER* for you to get here!"

At another time, Penelope might have pointed out that what Bob had said wasn't technically correct. But at that moment she was just relieved that Bob's crush didn't seem to be changing things between them.

"Oh my God," Bob said suddenly.

Penelope and Harry looked over to the courtyard, where Bob was pointing. Bob's dad was on the cotton candy stall. He was wearing a pink tutu over his jeans and waving around a stick of cotton candy to attract customers.

"He's KILLING me," Bob squealed, putting her hands around her own neck in a fake choking hold.

"I'M GOING TO DIE OF EMBARRASSMENT."

Penelope smiled. It was a real smile, because Bob was very funny. But, even though she wouldn't say it aloud, she was the one who was embarrassed. Bob's dad may have been wearing a tutu. But at least he was there.

"Where's your dad, Pen?" Bob asked. "I'm dying to know if he is even a teensy bit as wacky as mine."

Penelope gulped. Although Bob was her very best friend, Penelope wasn't ready to talk about what had happened to her family ties that morning.

"Something came up," she said.

Harry moved closer to Penelope. Shoulder to shoulder. And, even though he didn't say anything, Penelope knew what that meant.

Harry was being very caring. And that made Penelope feel emotional all over again. So it was probably just as well that Oscar Finley ran up to them just at that moment.

"I did the ten to ten thirty shift," he said. "Your Lucky Jars were going really well, Pen! I really reckon . . ." Oscar stopped midsentence as he noticed Penelope's brother.

"Hey, you're Harry Kingston! Jersey number sixteen?" he asked.

Harry nodded. "I've watched you play soccer," Oscar continued. "I was at the semifinal when you kicked three goals. You're awesome!"

Now it was Harry's turn to smile. And Penelope could tell it was a real smile, even if there was some sadness underneath it. Even if their own dad wouldn't be there to watch Harry play soccer and gush about it, at least someone would.

Just then, a huge roar came from the direction of the oval.

"Everyone's trying to dunk Mr. Joseph," Bob explained. "No one has managed it yet, but it'll be hilarious when it happens." Mr. Joseph was probably the grumpiest teacher in the whole of Chelsea Primary.

"Quick, everyone," Oscar said. "I've got a ripper of an idea."

The oval was full of amazing activities. There were pony rides, a jumping castle, and even a cup-and-saucer ride where you could sit inside a teacup and spin around. But the biggest crowd was around the Dunk Tank.

The Dunk Tank was made up of a see-through plastic tank filled with water. A seat was suspended above the tank, and on that seat was Mr. Joseph.

Next to the tank was a target with a hole in the center. That was the aim. If you got a ball to hit the target, the seat would sink—along with Mr. Joseph.

"Isn't anyone good enough to knock me off my perch?" Mr. Joseph challenged in his usual bellowing voice. "Just two dollars and you'll get your chance."

"I reckon you're the one to do it, Harry," Oscar said. "Jersey number sixteen, soccer legend, are you up for it?"

"You're all hopeless," Mr. Joseph yelled from the tank. "I'll be going home dry as a bone."

Harry narrowed his eyes and shook his head in a fake-fierce way. "Let's do this."

Oscar guided Harry to the front of the crowd. Harry paid his two dollars. Then, instead of holding the ball in his hands like everyone else had done, Harry put it at his feet.

Penelope pinched Bob on the thigh (because she absolutely knew you could do that with best friends when you were sharing a special moment).

The next bit was like slow motion. Harry brought his right foot back. He kicked. The ball flew through the air. Then it went straight into the target.

Mr. Joseph instantly went down. He flattened his (wet) nose against the window.

"Hero!" Oscar exclaimed, grabbing Harry's hand and lifting it into the air. Everyone cheered.

And Penelope realized something she'd never quite realized before.

Even if their dad didn't care, she was proud of her brother.

The rest of the day was so much fun, Penelope (almost) forgot about her outburst. Even Rita Azul was too busy having fun to think up a single mean thing to say. And, even though Tommy Stratton and Felix Unger did chase

her and Bob and let off fart bombs that smelled like rotten eggs (which was a very silly thing to do), Penelope didn't mind too much.

Penelope had:

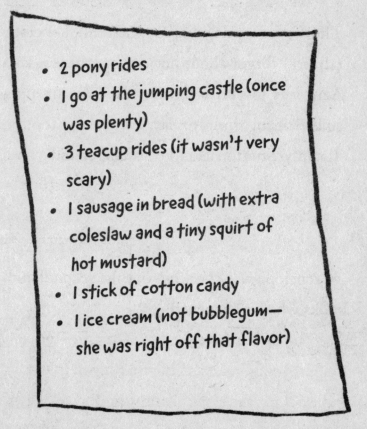

- 2 pony rides
- 1 go at the jumping castle (once was plenty)
- 3 teacup rides (it wasn't very scary)
- 1 sausage in bread (with extra coleslaw and a tiny squirt of hot mustard)
- 1 stick of cotton candy
- 1 ice cream (not bubblegum— she was right off that flavor)

It definitely wasn't a good day for the food pyramid, but despite a Truly Terrible start, it *was* a good day for Penelope.

It got even better when Penelope did her shift at the Lucky Jar stall. As soon as she'd sold the forty-fifth jar, she knew they'd done it. Penelope and Oscar found the principal and shared the good news.

Penelope (sweetly, and not saying a word about the time Ms. Bourke had forgotten to give Penelope an award for picking up litter without even being asked) reminded Ms. Bourke to make an announcement over the loudspeaker.

Penelope was checking out the secondhand books when it happened.

"The Lucky Jar record for Chelsea Primary has just been broken. A big thank-you to Oscar Finley and Penelope Kingston for all their great work!"

When Penelope had imagined this moment, she had pictured her dad right beside her, glowing with pride. But some moments are not how you imagine they'll be.

There were a couple of cheers, but most of the crowd kept doing whatever they were doing.

Around Penelope, though, a small group began to form. The group consisted of Oscar Finley, Bob, Harry, and Penelope's mum.

Oscar Finley high-fived her. Bob pinched her arm. Harry gave her two thumbs up, quite casually, but Penelope had a feeling that he was probably proud of her.

Penelope looked at her mum. Although she hadn't wanted to discuss it at the fair, she could tell that her mum knew what had happened with her dad. It was in her eyes. Penelope had a Strong Suspicion that her dad would be hearing from her mum about it. And that the words she used would be Very Pointy.

Then, without even trying, a Pleasant Image came to her.

THE IMAGE WAS OF HER MUM AS A FIERCE LIONESS, PROTECTING HER CUBS.

In front of everyone, Penelope's mum gave her a big hug.

"I am so crazily proud of you, Penelope Kingston," she whispered in Penelope's ear.

Normally, Penelope would have thought it was embarrassing to be hugged by her mum in public. This time, though, she didn't mind. **Not one bit.**

Sometimes, moments aren't exactly as you imagine they will be. But they can still be Very Special.

Just as Penelope was thinking that, her phone beeped. She assumed it would be Grandpa George. Grandpa often liked to find out whether his chart advice had worked.

Penelope wasn't sure how she was going to answer him.

Penelope's heart raced as she realized the text was from her father. It was the longest message she'd ever received.

Sweetheart. I've been thinking about what you said to me this morning. You're right. A promise isn't always given in words. I made a commitment to you and Harry and I have disappointed you both. Maybe, without realizing, I've been looking after my new family and not truly looking after you guys. I apologize. Please let me make it up to you and Harry. I want to be a good father. To all my kids.

P.S. I love you both.

P.P.S. I know that Sienna misses the five and the eight when she's trying to count to ten. The funny thing is, you did the same thing when you were her age too. It always makes me smile when she does that, because it reminds me of you.

Penelope handed the phone to her mum and Harry and watched as they read the message.

She truly wanted to believe her dad was going to change. But she was afraid to trust him.

"Did Dad make that up?" she asked her mum. "The bit about how I used to miss the five and the eight?"

Penelope's mum shook her head. "It's actually true," she said softly.

"Yeah," Harry agreed, "even I remember that. Dad used to correct you all the time."

Penelope closed her eyes. Perhaps Grandpa's chart had been right after all? Perhaps her (almost definitely) last outburst hadn't been *totally* the wrong thing to do?

She certainly couldn't remember her dad apologizing to her before. It felt new. In a good way. Like some mucky history had been washed away and now, perhaps, they could start afresh.

Penelope looked up from the text to her small but Very Special group.

"Are you okay, Poss?" her mum asked. Penelope glanced down at her mum's odd socks. Maybe in some ways she wasn't quite suited to her mum and Harry. But in other ways (no matter what happened with Penelope's dad) they were perfect together.

"I'm fine," Penelope said.

And, actually, she was.

PENELOPE KINGSTON HAS NEVER, EVER MESSED UP ON A TEST—UNTIL NOW.

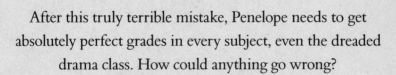

After this truly terrible mistake, Penelope needs to get absolutely perfect grades in every subject, even the dreaded drama class. How could anything go wrong?

CHRISSIE PERRY is the author of more than thirty books for children and young adults, including thirteen books in the popular Go Girl series and the award-winning *Whisper*. She lives in St. Kilda, Australia, with her husband and three children.

Like Penelope Kingston, Chrissie believes it's great to aim for excellence. But she also has a sneaking suspicion that going with the flow every now and then can also work out just fine.

PENELOPE KINGSTON IS ABSOLUTELY
certain that her stall at the school fair will be
a huge success. She and Oscar are in charge
of the lucky jars, and Penelope wants to break
last year's record.

This is even more important because
Penelope's dad is coming to the fair. She and
her brother, Harry, don't get to see him very
much these days, so Penelope is about to
burst with excitement. If she can make her dad
proud, maybe he'll want to spend every weekend with Penelope and Harry.

She just has to make sure everything goes
perfectly.

EVEN MORE
REASONS TO BE
PERFECT!

→

© 2017 BY MARTA KISSI · AGES 7–10 · 0517

Visit us at simonandschuster.com/kids